W9-BNU-743

Cinderella: the terrible truth

By Laura North

Illustrated by Joelle Dreidemy

Crabtree Publishing Company

www.crabtreebooks.com

Crabtree Publishing Company
www.crabtreebooks.com
1-800-387-7650

616 Welland Ave.
St. Catharines, ON
L2M 5V6

PMB 59051, 350 Fifth Ave.
59th Floor,
New York, NY 10118

Published by Crabtree Publishing Company in 2015

First published in 2012 by Franklin Watts
(A division of Hachette Children's Books)

Series editor: Melanie Palmer
Series advisor: Catherine Glavina
Series designer: Peter Scoulding
Editor: Kathy Middleton
Proofreader and notes to adults: Shannon Welbourn
Production coordinator and Prepress technician: Katherine Berti
Print coordinator: Katherine Berti

Printed in Hong Kong/082014/BK20140613

Library and Archives Canada Cataloguing in Publication

North, Laura, author
Cinderella : the terrible truth / by Laura North ; illustrated by Joelle Dreidemy.

(Race ahead with reading)
Issued in print and electronic formats.
ISBN 978-0-7787-1326-5 (bound).--
ISBN 978-0-7787-1327-2 (pbk.).--
ISBN 978-1-4271-7776-6 (pdf).--
ISBN 978-1-4271-7764-3 (html)

I. Dreidemy, Joelle, illustrator II. Title.

PZ7.N815Cin 2014 j823'.92 C2014-903678-7
C2014-903679-5

Library of Congress Cataloging-in-Publication Data

North, Laura.
Cinderella : the terrible truth / by Laura North ; illustrated by Joelle Dreidemy.
pages cm. -- (Race ahead with reading)
"First published in 2012 by Franklin Watts"--Copyright page.
ISBN 978-0-7787-1326-5 (reinforced library binding) -- ISBN 978-0-7787-1327-2 (pbk.) -- ISBN 978-1-4271-7776-6 (electronic pdf) -- ISBN 978-1-4271-7764-3 (electronic html)
[1. Fairy tales. 2. Princesses--Fiction. 3. Werewolves--Fiction.] I. Dreidemy, Joelle, illustrator. II. Title.
PZ8.N8117Ci 2014
[E]--dc23

2014020434

Chapter 1

Have you heard the story about Cinderella—the one where she wears rags and the Fairy Godmother turns her into a pretty princess?

Well, it's all a big cover-up.

That story hides the terrible truth.

Can you keep a secret?

It's true that Cinderella went to the famous royal ball.

"We've got an invitation to the Prince's ball," said one of her stepsisters.

"Do you want to go, Cinderella dear? You can borrow my dress."

"That's nice of you, sister!" said Cinderella, a little surprised because her stepsisters were usually so unkind to her. She took the beautiful dress and put it on.

"Drink this Cinderella," said her other stepsister.

"It's a love potion. It will make you even more beautiful, and the Prince will fall in love with you."

Cinderella, who was very trusting, said, "Thank you, sisters, you are so kind!"

She drank the potion in one gulp.

But her stepsisters were not kind. They were cruel, mean, and jealous of her beauty.

It was certainly not a love potion.

But what was it?

Chapter 2

"We're here!" cried the stepsisters as they arrived at the palace with Cinderella. A full moon lit up her beautiful blue dress. "You look wonderful," they told her.

"Wow!" said the Prince, as he stared at Cinderella. "You are beautiful!"

Cinderella looked behind her. Surely the Prince didn't mean her. But he dashed right up to her.

"The potion is working!" she thought. "It has made me beautiful."

The Prince fell so madly in love with her he wanted to marry her that very night.

"Cinderella, you must marry me now! I cannot let you get away."

So they were married right away.

Cinderella became a princess.

The ball became a wedding party.

What could ruin such a perfect night?

Chapter 3

"BONG! BONG! BONG!"

The clock struck midnight. Outside, the big, round full moon shone brightly.

But Cinderella's beautiful dress did not turn back into rags. Instead, the potion began its terrible work.

The Prince gazed deeply into the eyes of his new love. “Cinderella,” he said, “you have such big, beautiful eyes.”

“Oh, Prince, thank you,” said Cinderella.

"Cinderella..." said the Prince,
pausing, as he brushed
his fingers over her hair.
"You really do have
tremendously big ears."

Cinderella liked the Prince,
but his comments were
getting a bit personal.
"Well, Prince, I hadn't
really noticed," she replied.

"Cinderella," said the Prince, now speaking very slowly. "I hadn't noticed what great big teeth you have."

"Now, that's just rude," thought Cinderella.

But Cinderella thought that she should be polite to her new husband.

"It is so I can smile at you all the better," she told him. And she gave the biggest smile that she had ever given.

The Prince looked at her and screamed. Cinderella called after the Prince as he ran out of the palace.

Chapter 4

"What's happening?" cried Cinderella.

All around her, the guests were screaming.

"It's disgusting!" shouted one lady, pointing at Cinderella. "Save us!"

"What's wrong?" asked Cinderella, running toward her. The woman screamed and jumped out of the window into the moat. In the night sky, the moon glowed full and round.

A servant yelled,

"Look at those big, ugly feet!

And those terrible claws!"

Cinderella looked down.

Underneath her beautiful dress

a pair of huge, hairy feet poked out.

Her hands had

long, twisted

fingernails.

She went to the middle of the ballroom

to look in a mirror.

"Help! I'm a monster!" she cried.

Her whole body was covered in thick hair,

and her face was furry with fierce fangs

and a snout. She was a werewolf!

"Not so pretty now, Cinderella!" laughed one of her mean stepsisters.

"And you thought it was a love potion!"

The sisters stopped laughing when

Cinderella leaped toward them.

When all the guests had run away, Cinderella stood alone in the middle of the ballroom and howled.

Chapter 5

Five years later, Cinderella sat locked in a cage. "This is my prison," she said as she looked at the bars.

But she was not alone.

The Prince sat next

to her cage.

"Well, we do have

to keep you locked up

when there's a full moon.

We don't want you to eat

any more of our relatives."

On the night of the ball, Cinderella had quickly gobbled up her two stepsisters.

The Prince still loved her. It had been a shock to find out she was a werewolf. But he didn't mind a bit of hairiness and a bad temper.

At bedtime, their three children lay around him. “Daddy,” said the small boy. “Why is mommy locked in a cage?”
“I’ll tell you why when you’re a bit older, son,” he said.

The Royal Family, however, wanted to keep it all a secret. So they made up a wonderful story about a Fairy Godmother,

...a pumpkin,

...and a magic spell.

As strange as that story was, it was hard to imagine that the truth was even stranger.

But I know the true story.

And now so do you.

Don't tell *anyone* else...

Notes for Adults

These entertaining, first chapter books help children build up their reading skills so they can move on to longer books. Fun illustrations and bite-sized chapters encourage young readers to take the driver's seat and ***Race Ahead with Reading.***

THE FOLLOWING BEFORE, DURING, AND AFTER READING ACTIVITY SUGGESTIONS SUPPORT LITERACY SKILL DEVELOPMENT AND CAN ENRICH SHARED READING EXPERIENCES:

BEFORE

1. Make reading fun! Choose a time to read when you and the reader are relaxed and have time to share the story together. Don't forget to give praise! Children learn best in a positive environment.

2. Before reading, ask the reader to look at the title and illustration on the cover of the book **Cinderella: the terrible truth**. Invite them to make predictions about what will happen in the story. They may make use of prior knowledge and make connections to other stories they have heard or read about Cinderella or another similar character.

DURING

3. Encourage readers to determine unfamiliar words themselves by using clues from the text and illustrations.

4. During reading, encourage the child to review his or her understanding and see if they want to revise their predictions midway. Encourage the reader to make text-to-text connections, choosing a part of the story that reminds them of another story they have read; and text-to-self connections, choosing a part of the story that relates to their own personal experiences; and text-to-world connections, choosing a part of the story that reminds them of something that happened in the real world.

AFTER

5. Ask the reader who the main characters are in this story. Have the child retell the story in their own words. Ask him or her to think about the predictions they made before reading the story. How were they the same or different?

DISCUSSION QUESTIONS FOR KIDS

6. Throughout this story, Cinderella has some unexpected things occur. How does Cinderella or other characters react to these surprising events and challenges?

7. Choose one of the illustrations from the story. How do the details in the picture help you understand a part of the story better? Or, what do they tell you that is not in the text?

8. What part of the story surprised you? Why was it a surprise?

9. The stepsisters were not kind to Cinderella. Why do you think Cinderella trusted them when they offered her the fancy dress and love potion?

10. What moral, or lesson, can you take from this story?

11. Create your own story or drawing about something unexpected that happened to you and how you responded to it.